D1217512

# STONE MEN

## by NICKI WEISS

Greenwillow Books  New York

Pastels and colored pencils were used for the full-color art.
The text type is Windsor Old Style Light.
Copyright © 1993 by Monica J. Weiss. All rights reserved. No part of this
book may be reproduced or utilized in any form or by any means, electronic
or mechanical, including photocopying, recording, or by any information
storage and retrieval system, without permission in writing from the
Publisher, Greenwillow Books, a division of William Morrow & Company, Inc.,
1350 Avenue of the Americas, New York, NY 10019.
Printed in Hong Kong by South China Printing Company (1988) Ltd.
First Edition  10 9 8 7 6 5 4 3 2 1

Library of Congress Cataloging-in-Publication Data

Weiss, Nicki.
Stone men / by Nicki Weiss.
p.  cm.
Summary: Grandma tells Arnie how a poor peddler saved a
village from with being destroyed by soldiers with the help
of the stone men he always made on his journeys.
ISBN 0-688-11015-0 (trade). ISBN 0-688-11016-9 (lib.)
[1. Peddlers and peddling—Fiction.    2. Jews—Fiction.
3. Grandmothers—Fiction.]    I. Title.
CURR  PZ7.W448145St    1993
[E]—dc20    92-3959    CIP    AC

IN MEMORY OF MY GRANDPARENTS
THEODORE AND VILMA
JOSEPH AND GERTRUDE

Arnie sat on his grandmother's lap. "Tell me a story, Grandma," he said.

"You mean the one about Reuben the candlemaker?" Grandma asked.

"No, no," Arnie said. "Another one."

"How about the one with Freda the watchmaker's wife and her three daughters?" Grandma asked.

"No, Grandma," said Arnie. "A new story. One you never told before."

"All right," Grandma said. She thought a moment and began....

"There once was a peddler named Isaac. He was a poor peddler, with nothing but a cart to his name. There had been a time when Isaac owned a mule, but that was a long time ago.

"The mule died of old age, and Isaac was too poor to

buy a new one. So he took to pushing his own cart
over the miles and miles from one isolated village to
another. From Glovotno to Presno, from Freiberg to
Slovitski, from Hullitch to Koralevka, Isaac slowly
and steadily pushed the cart.

"When Isaac would finally reach a village, everyone
was glad to see him. After all, his cart was filled
with all the knickknacks, doodads, and gewgaws
they needed. Laces and linens, pots and pans,
nails and buttons, old shoes and new underwear.
You name it, Isaac had it.
'Got any beeswax, Isaac?' asked Benny the baker.
'How about a corkscrew, Isaac?' asked Minnie the
cheesemaker's wife.

"Isaac would silently hand over the items and accept the money they gave him. Sometimes he'd give a child a little stone man he'd made on his journey. Then he'd turn his cart in the direction of the next village and move on.
'Strange fellow,' Otto the butcher would say.
'Never talks,' Max the horse trader would add.
'All those years alone on the plains have made him a little peculiar,' Lena the milkman's daughter would comment.

"Maybe Isaac was a little peculiar.
Over the years he spent less and less
time with people and more and more
time trekking across the distances from
village to village.
And always, as soon as he left a
village, as soon as he could no longer
see a house or a person or a farm
animal, Isaac would stop his cart. He
would start looking for stones—large
ones, small ones.

"Then he'd pile them up.
He might add a branch or two.
He might add an old rag from his cart.
And presto! A man made of stone!

"As Isaac continued on his way, pushing the cart
along, he would look back from time to time.
And there stood the stone man, a patient friend
eternally waiting. A friend to talk to. Maybe
not a friend who answered back, but a friend
nonetheless, someone who listened to what was
in Isaac's heart.

"And as Isaac continued on, and the distance
between them grew, it became harder and harder
to see his friend… until he could see him no more.
Then Isaac would stop and gather some stones.
He'd pile one on top of the other.
He'd maybe add some tumbleweed.
Perhaps an old hat from the cart.
And presto! Another stone man to talk to for miles
to come.
And so on and on. From stone man to stone man.
That's how Isaac made his way from one village
to the next.

"Now, as fate would have it, Isaac arrived in the village of Bruria as the holiday of Passover was approaching.

'I need a large pot, Isaac,' Esther the rabbi's wife said.

'How about some black thread, Isaac?' requested Abe the tailor.

'Did you hear about what happened in Vlisk?' Mordecai the scribe asked the group surrounding the cart.

'What?' they replied in unison.

'The czar's soldiers came and ransacked the village. Turned it upside down,' Mordecai said.

'If they ransacked one village,' Abe said, 'you may be sure they'll destroy another.'

"Isaac silently handed over the things the villagers bought.
He gave a child a little stone man he'd made on his journey,
and turned his cart in the direction of the next village.
The villagers watched until Isaac and the cart were out
of sight.

'Such an odd man,' Abe the tailor said.

'A quiet one, I'll say,' added the rabbi's wife.

'Doesn't seem to need a person in the world,' said Mordecai
the scribe. 'I wouldn't want to have to depend on him for
anything more than the wares in his cart.'

"Isaac walked on his way. He built a stone man and
continued walking. After a while he built another.
On he traveled.
The sun set at the edge of the plain, and darkness
gathered around him.
Isaac was about to unload the bedroll from his cart
for a good night's rest when he saw a flickering
light up ahead. He listened, and he could hear voices.
Isaac left the cart and went closer to have a look.

"From behind a tree he saw a group of soldiers
sitting around a roaring campfire!

"'At dawn we'll ride up to Bruria before they have a chance
to know what's going on,' he heard someone say.
'We'll take the village by storm!' was the last thing Isaac
heard before he ran off.

"Only the light of the moon lit Isaac's path. Past the cart he flew. Past the stone men he had built earlier that same day. When Isaac finally arrived in Bruria, not a light was shining in any window. Not a soul was awake. It was only a few days before Passover, and everyone in the village was exhausted from cleaning, cooking, fixing, mending, putting away winter clothes, and taking out holiday dishes.

Isaac ran to the first door he saw and knocked. No one answered. He ran next door. There wasn't a sound to be heard.

No time to waste, Isaac thought, and he ran on.

"It was still dark when Mordecai the scribe awoke.
'Hoofbeats!' Mordecai cried to his wife. He jumped
out of bed, and sure enough, there was a slight
trembling of the earth beneath his feet.

"Mordecai ran out of the house and into the street,
shouting, 'Wake up, everybody! The czar's soldiers
are coming!'
In no time at all people were awake and running
through the village. 'What shall we do?' they cried.

"Alas, there wasn't much to do. There was no time for
running away or for planning a defense of any kind.
'They must have waited for just the right moment,' said
Simon the grain dealer, 'to see by the light of dawn.'
For there, right at the edge of the hills that surrounded
their village, was the beginning of an orange glow.

"The hoofbeats were getting louder, and the villagers
could just make out in the growing light the movement
of mounted soldiers coming toward them.
'Nothing can save this village now,' cried the cobbler's
daughter.
'What we need,' said the rabbi, 'is a miracle.'

"Just then there was a faint sweep of morning light, and the sun peeked over the hills. Suddenly, as the villagers watched in amazement, the soldiers drew in their reins and pulled their horses up short. There was confusion and disarray. The horses ran in different directions. And then they all turned and galloped away!
The villagers could hardly believe what they saw.
'You'd think they'd seen a ghost,' said Benny the baker.
'Or a dybbuk,' Masha the midwife said.
'Or Elijah,' the rabbi said.

"'Look!' shouted Abe the tailor, and everyone followed
his pointing finger.
There on the ridge of the hills around them stood a
row of stone men. In the dim light it looked as if
there was an army defending the little village.

"And that's the story of how Isaac saved the village of Bruria," Grandma said.

"Did it really happen, Grandma?" Arnie asked.

Grandma reached over to the bookcase. She took something from a shelf. She handed it to Arnie.

"Presto!" Grandma said. "A man made of stone."

"Just like the one Isaac gave that child in your story!" Arnie said.

"The very one," said Grandma.

"So you were that child," Arnie said.

"And I saw everything with my own eyes," replied Grandma.

"But what happened to Isaac?" Arnie asked.

"Well, of course a big fuss was made over Isaac when it became known what he had done. He was an honored guest at the rabbi's table on Passover. For the entire week of the holiday Isaac was treated like a king.

"But then the holiday was over.
And although Oscar the merchant and Abe the tailor
tried to talk him into staying in Bruria forever, Isaac
got his cart, nodded his head good-bye, and pointed
the cart in the direction of the next village. He walked
on his way.

"And when he could no longer see Bruria, Isaac stopped the cart. He found some stones—large ones, small ones. He piled them up. He added a moth-eaten glove from his cart.
And presto! A stone man.
Then Isaac traveled on, talking to his friend, until he couldn't see him anymore."